THE TALKING
LIZARD

Written by **Pat Rynearson**
Illustrated by **Roxanne Ressler**

At night I lie in bed and listen to the darkness.

"Geck-o! Geck-o!" I hear.

"Who is that talking?" I ask.

Then I see the small shape on the wall.

It is a little lizard, telling me its name.

I say, "My name is Mai-Li."

The lizard doesn't answer me,

but I know it is my friend, the gecko.

No other lizard would tell me its name.

We had geckos in my village in China.

We have them here, too, in my new home.

Night is my favorite time.

It is the gecko's favorite time, too.

People noises are still, but the night is not.

I hear crickets and the happy sound of their wings rubbing together.

I hear the high singing of mosquitoes.

I see the shadowy shape of the gecko.

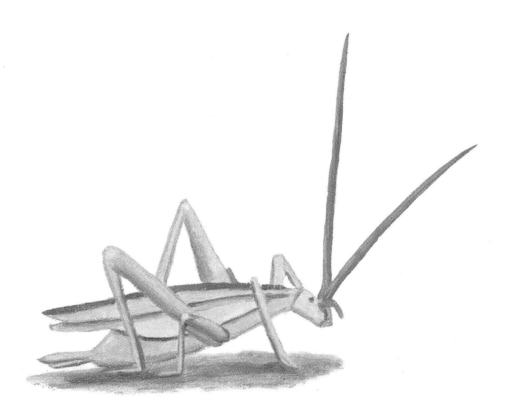

Some people might be afraid to have a gecko in their room.

I am not.

I know the gecko is my friend.

I watch it walk right up the window.

The suction pads on its feet keep it from falling.

Now it is hanging upside down from the ceiling.

I laugh.

What a wonderful trick!

It is hard to see my little gecko in the dark,

but I can hear its voice talking to me.

"Geck-o! Geck-o!" it says.

"I know, I know, you silly thing," I whisper.

"You have already told me your name."

The gecko dashes across the room.

"Where did you go?" I ask, following the sound of its
voice in the dark.

I can't see many things at night,

but the gecko's large, round eyes see very well.

There it is, in the moonlit corner of my room.

It must have something in its eye.

It uses its long, sticky tongue like a windshield wiper.

I like my little gecko friend.

It feasts on those pesky mosquitoes that sing around my ears.

In China, we believe geckos bring good luck.

I know I am truly lucky to have one in my room.

Wouldn't you like to have a gecko in yours?